The Greenwood Adventurers

Written by
Amanda Brandon

Illustrated by
Agnieszka Potocka

Chapter 1

Crunch! Marian took the last bite of her apple and flicked the core. She perched in a tree, one leg dangling over a branch. Her dress was ripped and her hair had twigs sticking out, but Marian didn't care. She was too busy staying out of sight.

She picked another apple and munched again. The sound of horses' hooves grew fainter. At last! Her father's visitor had gone. She could climb down now. She flicked away the last core and heard a loud **"Ouch!"**

She peered through the branches. Oops! It was her father, Lord Fitzwaters. He didn't look pleased. "Marian! Get down at once. This behaviour is most unladylike." Marian slowly slid down the branch. "Good gracious! Look at the state of you. What would your mother say if she were alive today to see you?"

"Sorry, Father." Marian scuffed the ground with her boot.

"I need to travel abroad on important business," her father said. "So I have decided you will go away to school. Lady Jennifer has an establishment for young noblewomen called Greenwood. It sounds perfect."

"School?!" Marian pouted. "Why would I want to go *there?* Can't I stay home? I promise not to be any trouble."

"Hmm... You and trouble go together like bread and jam." Lord Fitzwaters snorted but his eyes twinkled. "No. I've made up my mind."

"Please, they'll make me do needlework and you know how bad I am at that. My stitches are always wonky." Marian threw her arms around her father and gave her most dazzling smile. "Pleeease, let me stay home."

Lord Fitzwaters pushed her gently away and said, "Perhaps it's about time you learned how to behave like a lady."

"No! I won't go to school! I won't!" This time, instead of pleading, Marian stamped her foot.

"That's enough! You are going and that's the end of it. Now, I must prepare for my trip and so must you." Lord Fitzwaters turned and strode back towards the house.

Marian sobbed and pounded her fists against the old apple tree she had climbed earlier. Then she hugged the thick trunk, feeling the rough bark rub her cheek. Her beloved climbing tree; she would miss it because of some stupid school. It wasn't fair.

Chapter 2

A few days later, Marian climbed in a cart, waved her father goodbye and set off. The horses charged ahead. "These horses want me to arrive as soon as possible," she grumbled. She tried not to think about the fate that awaited her. Finally, the steady clatter of hooves lulled her to sleep.

She woke suddenly when she was tipped to the other side of the cart. She heard loud, frantic neighs and shouts. Her father's servant, Henry, had veered off the road. He shook his fist at the figure dressed in dark clothes who overtook them. "Wretched Sheriff!" she heard Henry mutter.

He reset the cart and they continued, but Marian shivered as she remembered the fierce figure of the Sheriff as he sped by on his horse.

The sun had sunk low by the time they slowed down. The path had narrowed and it was hard to see ahead through the canopy of trees. Then, around the bend, Marian saw Greenwood. The half-timber manor house was almost completely hidden from the road.

Marian was met by a tall woman with flame-red hair tied at the nape of her neck. She wore a long cloak which swished as she moved.

"I'm Lady Jennifer. Welcome to Greenwood. I expect you're tired after your long journey." She beckoned to a small, fair-haired girl. "Scarlet, show Marian to the sleeping quarters please."

"Yes, Lady Jennifer." The little girl grinned at Marian who noticed a gap in the girl's two front teeth.

She followed her up the winding staircase. Henry had been given orders to leave Marian's belongings in the hall for someone to fetch later.

"Well, here we are," Scarlet said as she showed Marian to a small room. "This is your bed," she added, pointing to one by the window. "And that's mine." She sat on the second one by the wall. "I hope we'll be friends."

"Maybe. But I won't be staying long," Marian said with more confidence than she felt. "I don't want to learn how to arrange flowers or sew."

Scarlet burst out laughing.

"What's so funny?" Marian snapped.

"We don't do any of that here!" Scarlet said. "Didn't you know? Greenwood is special. We sometimes have to put on dancing displays for visitors, but Lady Jennifer teaches us how to fire a bow and arrow, and to fish!"

Marian's frown disappeared and her eyes lit up. "You mean...?"

"Yes!" Scarlet was clearly delighted at Marian's surprise. "All our lessons take place in the woods!"

Chapter 3

Marian's first days at Greenwood passed in a blur.
There were archery lessons, and they learnt how to
tie knots and building the perfect shelters with the
strongest branches.

Cook, a stout woman, showed them how to forage
for food and recognise poisonous plants and fungi.
Later, they roasted their tastier finds over a fire they
had built themselves.

There were eight pupils—or 'adventurers' as Lady
Jennifer preferred to call them—at Greenwood, and

they were all sworn not to reveal the true nature of their activities.

"If word got out, Lady Jennifer would be in trouble with the Sheriff," Scarlet told Marian.

"I would never tell!" Marian remembered the angry-looking man she had seen a few days earlier and added, "I thought school would be dull, but lessons at Greenwood are fun."

One early evening, they headed for the woods because Lady Jennifer said that was the best time for tracks to show.

She told them to find an animal's trail and added, "You will need to look for broken cobwebs or droppings, some flattened grass too."

They divided into pairs and set off. Marian teamed up with Scarlet and, together, they peered at the ground to try and spot the prints of a deer.

"I can't see anything," Marian grumbled after they'd walked for a while.

"Me neither." Scarlet sighed. "I didn't realise it would be this hard."

Marian sat on a log and rubbed her sore feet. Scarlet joined her. Suddenly, they heard a loud hoot. Scarlet shrieked.

"It's only an owl," Marian said, although the sound had startled her too.

The hooting continued. Scarlet whispered, "I don't like this."

Marian scanned the trees. It was growing dark. She couldn't see far. She stepped towards a clump of bushes. "I think it's coming from over here."

A second hoot sounded from a branch further

away. "No! It's over there!" Scarlet pointed.

Marian rushed over but she couldn't see anything. Hooting came from behind her again. Surely the owl couldn't be in two places at once. They would have heard the flap of wings.

Marian stood still. She heard a giggle and rustle of leaves. "That's no bird," she said. "There's someone there. Come out, whoever you are! Stop playing games."

Something pinged her ear. "Ow!" It was an acorn. Marian scowled and reached for her bow and arrow. Next time she saw movement, she would fire and scare whatever it was away.

There was another

rustle. Marian drew her bow and pulled.

Zap! The arrow flew through the air. They

heard an "Oi!" followed by a thud.

Marian and Scarlet rushed to the bushes. A boy

about their age was sprawled on his back with his

eyes closed.

"You've killed him!" Scarlet gasped.

Chapter 4

The boy opened his eyes and smirked. "Not with that shot she didn't!"

"Agreed!" Marian said. "I aimed at the tree to scare you."

"These bushes are very prickly by the way," the boy said. "Help me up?"

Marian crossed her arms. "No, it serves you right. You were trying to scare us."

The boy grinned again. "Sorry. I couldn't resist. I saw you peering at the path and decided to play a joke. Why are you out here so late?"

"We're staying with Lady Jennifer," Scarlet said. Marian shot her a warning look. "And err... we just wanted a walk after supper."

"What are *you* doing here?" Marian asked. "And who are you?"

"My name's Robin. I live with a couple of friends here. These are my woods." He opened his arms wide.

"No, they're not. They belong to Lady Jennifer," Marian glared. Robin's cocky manner was so annoying!

He said with a cheerful grin, "I know Lady Jennifer: she always lets me use the woods."

Marian wasn't convinced. Robin leant back on the tree trunk and looked up at the arrow she had fired earlier. He seemed too confident for her liking, and she could still feel the sting of the acorn.

"Well, don't play tricks on us again! Come on, Scarlet, we're going." She grabbed her friend's arm.

"Of course, your ladyship." Robin bowed but he was still grinning.

Marian huffed. "I hope that's the last we see of him." But she had a feeling that it wouldn't be.

Chapter 5

When they returned to the clearing, the other adventurers were already with Lady Jennifer.

Marian thought Lady Jennifer would be cross but she simply said, "If you must fire your bow, Marian, at least put it away properly."

Marian hastily did as she was told and they returned to the Manor House. Lady Jennifer told the others to prepare for bed, but she called Marian back. "How are you settling into Greenwood?"

"I miss my father and my special climbing tree but, now I'm here, I love exploring the woodland, and our lessons are amazing."

Lady Jennifer smiled. "Good, I'm glad."

"Why did you decide to open Greenwood?" Marian was suddenly curious as to why the lady of the manor would do such a thing.

"Ah well, my brother who truly owns the place is away fighting with for the king. We grew up together playing in these woods." Lady Jennifer looked across at the swishing trees surrounding the house and her voice became wistful. She added, "One day, we were attacked by robbers and my brother was injured. He recovered but I never forgot how I was powerless to help him. I vowed that no one would make me feel like that again."

Marian nodded, thinking how frightened Lady Jennifer must have been.

Lady Jennifer continued, "I never want other young girls to feel the way I felt. I want them to be brave, but always think wisely too."

Marian reddened at the thought of how she'd fired the arrow at Robin because she was annoyed.

She said she was aiming at the tree but what if she *had* hit him? She vowed to think before she used her bow too quickly in the future.

A few days later, everyone was practising archery in the woods when Cook came dashing out.

"The Sheriff has arrived! Quick! You must look presentable."

The adventurers sped back to the manor. They knew that if a visitor came, they were to sit in the Great Hall and pick up their sewing.

But before they reached the main doors, they had to jump out of the way of the Sheriff's coach and horses hurtling down the path away from the school.

"Watch out!" Marian gasped as the Sheriff whipped his horses faster.

"Look!" Scarlet cried as they glimpsed a pale face with flaming red hair. "He's kidnapped Lady Jennifer! What are we going to do?"

Chapter 6

"It's all my fault." Marian sobbed. "I bet it was that Robin we met in the woods the other day. He was probably cross after I shot an arrow, and he told the Sheriff."

Cook looked surprised. "It can't possibly be Robin."

"Why not?"

"Robin is Lady Jennifer's nephew. He's devoted to her. He would never do anything to get her into trouble."

"So that's why he's allowed to roam the woods! No wonder he looked so smug." Marian smacked a hand to her forehead.

Cook wrung her hands. "Oh dear! Whatever are we to do? Perhaps you ought to pack and I'll make arrangements for your families to collect you."

There was a cry of dismay.

"We're not leaving Greenwood!" Marian said. "Lady Jennifer needs us! First, we need a plan. I'm going to the woods to find Robin. I suggest everyone eats a good meal. We're going to be very busy."

Before Cook could protest, Marian ran into the woods. She worried for Lady Jennifer. Where would the Sheriff take her? Perhaps Robin might know. She didn't want to ask, but he was the only one who might be able to help.

She reached the clearing where they had met a few days ago and found a large oak tree to climb. It reminded her of her special tree at home. She rested in its branches and a plan began to form. A short while later, she cupped her hands to her lips and tried to hoot like an owl, just as Robin had done. It sounded more like a pigeon. She tried again.

This time, a hoot came back. It was the middle of the afternoon: it had to be Robin.

She slid down the tree and looked about. She felt someone's hands over her eyes. "Guess who?" a playful voice sang.

Marian ducked away. "This is no time for games, Robin! Lady Jennifer has been kidnapped. I need your help to find her."

Robin gasped. Marian told him what had happened.

"The Sheriff would have taken her to his castle on the other side of the village. But you'll never pass the guards on your own. It's too dangerous."

"I must. I've got to save her!"

"No, she's *my* aunt—I'll go."

"We'll do it together," Marian said firmly. "Listen carefully, I've got a plan."

Chapter 7

After some discussion, Marian and Robin returned to Greenwood and explained their plan to the rest of the adventurers. Early next morning, Cook gave Marian a basket of freshly baked buns. Then Marian set off through the woods with Robin.

They followed the marks of the Sheriff's horses. "You're better at tracking than me," Marian admitted as Robin noted where the grass had been flattened.

"I've had plenty of practice. You'll manage it too after a while," he said.

Soon, they came to the edge of the wood and saw the castle in the distance.

"Good luck!" Robin said.

Marian nodded. She headed towards the castle gates, holding the basket of buns.

She held them out to a guard who told her to stop. "The Sheriff ordered them fresh from the village."

The guard peered at her. "Hmm..."

Marian flashed her most winning smile. "Here, try

one." She lifted the cloth, making sure to keep her bow and arrow hidden underneath. Then she handed him a bun.

"Well, I *am* hungry. I've been on duty all night. Mmm... these are good." He took a bite. "Very well. You may go through."

He opened the gate. Marian turned and tossed him another bun. As he scrambled to catch it, Robin slipped in behind Marian, unnoticed.

Chapter 8

"Where might Lady Jennifer be?" Marian whispered as they headed for the kitchen. They removed their bows and arrows and hid the basket.

"Try here!" Robin pointed to some steps. "These lead to the dungeons. Be careful no one catches you. As soon as you find her, make for the west wall of the castle. I'll be waiting."

Marian hurried down the steps. She peered into every nook she could see, ignoring the shadows which darted on the cold stone walls.

"Lady Jennifer," she whispered. "Are you there?"

Finally, at the end of the row, a small voice cried, "Over here."

Marian tried the heavy door but it was locked. "Hold on! I'll find the key." She hunted around but couldn't find anything.

Marian tried to pick the lock with the tip of an arrow but it was no use. She was wondering what to do next when she heard footsteps. "That's the guard bringing breakfast," Lady Jennifer said. "Quick, you must hide!"

Marian slipped into an alcove, but it had given her an idea. The guard unlocked Lady Jennifer's door and entered. He knelt to put down the plate. Marian charged forwards and shoved him with her shoulder. **OOF!** The guard was knocked off balance.

He tried to rise but Lady Jennifer, who was tied to a chair, stuck out her foot and tripped him. As he fell, his head hit the stone wall of the dungeon. He sank to the floor, knocked out.

Marian untied Lady Jennifer and used the ropes to tie up the guard. "There! Now he won't be able to raise the alarm when he wakes up," she said.

"Impressive knots, Marian," Lady Jennifer nodded in approval. "But we must hurry. The other guards will be suspicious when he fails to return."

Together, they raced up the stairs. "We need to head for the west side," Marian panted.

At the west wall, Robin was waiting for them. He had tied a rope which dropped to the ground outside the castle. "The adventurers are creating a commotion on the east side of the castle just as we

asked them to. Hurry! The guards are distracted."

Lady Jennifer climbed down first. She beckoned to Marian to follow. Soon, she joined her at the bottom. Robin started to climb too when Marian cried, **"Look out!"**

The Sheriff swaggered towards him. His mouth was pulled into a snarl. He shouted "You may have escaped this time, Lady Jennifer, but one day I'll make Greenwood Manor mine."

Lady Jennifer shouted, "Never! I won't be your bargaining tool."

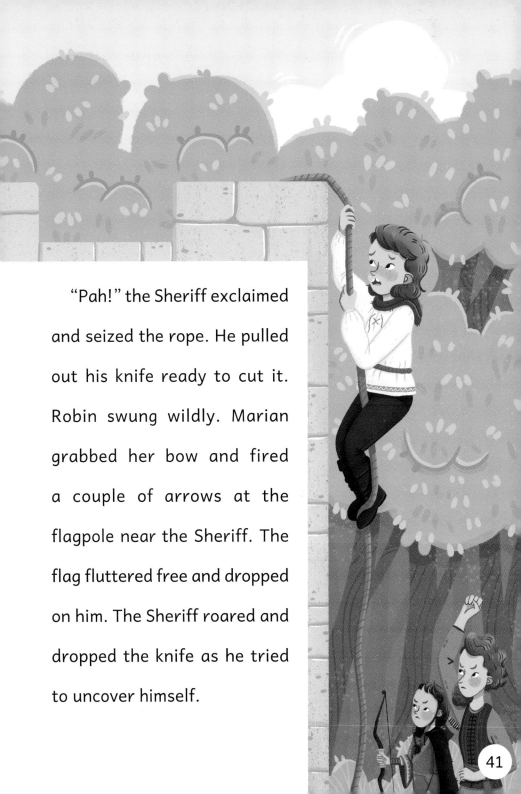

"Pah!" the Sheriff exclaimed and seized the rope. He pulled out his knife ready to cut it. Robin swung wildly. Marian grabbed her bow and fired a couple of arrows at the flagpole near the Sheriff. The flag fluttered free and dropped on him. The Sheriff roared and dropped the knife as he tried to uncover himself.

"Hurry!" Marian and Lady Jennifer shouted. Robin scrambled down.

They fled into the woods, where the trees kept them safely hidden.

Later, everyone reunited at the Manor. Lady Jennifer explained, "The Sheriff took me because he thought my brother would give up Greenwood Manor in exchange for my safe return, but his plan failed."

"Lady Jennifer was so brave!" Marian told the others. "She didn't let the Sheriff get away with his mean tricks."

"Do you think the Sheriff will return now he knows what we've been learning?" Scarlet's lip wobbled.

Lady Jennifer said, "Don't worry. Now we know

the Sheriff's plan we can be on our guard. The Greenwood Adventurers have proved they are more than a match for him!"

Marian was ready to fight for Greenwood. She had found friends and a new place to call home there!

Suddenly, they heard a clamour of hooves.

"Surely the Sheriff hasn't returned!" Marian's voice rose in alarm.

Lady Jennifer leapt up and ran to the window. "It's my brother." She put her finger to her lips and added, "Shh! Don't mention the Sheriff's kidnap attempt."

Lady Jennifer's brother entered the room and nodded his approval at the circle of girls quietly stitching and Robin lounging by the fireside.

"I just saw the most extraordinary thing at the castle," he said.

"What's that?" Lady Jennifer asked, pouring him some refreshment.

"My men and I went to see the Sheriff on official business and when we arrived he was stomping up and down and shouting. There had obviously been a fight but when I asked what happened he turned bright red and refused to say another word."

Lady Jennifer gave them all a wink and said, "Well, I never!"

Marian grinned at Robin. It looked like the Sheriff had been too embarrassed to admit being beaten by them. He would think twice about messing with the Greenwood Adventurers in the future!

Discussion Points

1. Where is Marian at the beginning of the story?

2. What do the girls at Greenwood *not* learn to do?

a) Shoot a bow and arrow

b) Make dresses

c) Forage for food

3. What was your favourite part of the story?

4. What sound does Marian make to get Robin's attention?

5. Why do you think Marian liked the lessons at Greenwood?

6. Who was your favourite character and why?

7. There were moments in the story when Marian and Robin had to **work together**. Where do you think the story shows this most?

8. What do you think happens after the end of the story?

Book Bands for Guided Reading

The Institute of Education book banding system is a scale of colours that reflects the various levels of reading difficulty. The bands are assigned by taking into account the content, the language style, the layout and phonics. Word, phrase and sentence level work is also taken into consideration.

The Maverick Readers Scheme is a bright, attractive range of books covering the pink to grey bands. All of these books have been book banded for guided reading to the industry standard and edited by a leading educational consultant.

To view the whole Maverick Readers scheme, visit our website at

www.maverickearlyreaders.com

Or scan the QR code to view our scheme instantly!

Maverick Chapter Readers
(From Lime to Grey Band)